The Amazing Paper Book

Written by
Paulette Bourgeois

Illustrated by
Linda Hendry

Kids Can Press Ltd.
Toronto

Kids Can Press Ltd. gratefully acknowledges the assistance of the Canada Council and the Ontario Arts Council in the production of this book.

Canadian Cataloguing in Publication Data

Bourgeois, Paulette
    The amazing paper book

Includes index.
ISBN 0-921103-82-4

1. Paper - Juvenile literature. 2. Papermaking - Juvenile literature. 3. Paper work - Juvenile literature. I. Hendry, Linda. II. Title.

TS1105.5.B68 1989   j676'.2   C89-093181-X

Edited by Valerie Wyatt
Book design by Michael Solomon
Typeset by Alphabets
Printed and bound in Canada

89   0 9 8 7 6 5 4 3 2 1

Contents

Paper makes the world go round 6
Why we need paper 8
Write on! 12
Getting from A to B
  (Alphabet to Book) 14
Modern paper inventions 18
Paper firsts 20
Make your own paper 26
Nature's papermakers 30
Learning from the wasp 32
Paper puzzlers 34
Pioneer loggers 42
Tall tales of the lumberjacks 46
Ask a forester 51
Take a tour through a paper mill 58
Making a newspaper 64
Second-hand paper 66
Answers 76
Glossary 77
Index 79

Acknowledgements

This book would not have been possible
without the information provided by The
Canadian Pulp and Paper Association,
Abitibi Price Inc., Crown Forest Industries,
the Council of Forest Industries of British
Columbia, the Canadian Forestry
Association, E.B. Eddy Forest Products
Ltd. and the American Paper Institute. The
Royal Ontario Museum, the Ontario Science
Centre and Pollution Probe provided
information about forestry, insects, papermaking and the environment. I am grateful
to Dr. Paul L. Aird of the University of
Toronto's School of Forestry for reading
the manuscript and making so many
valuable suggestions. Finally, a thanks to
my favourite editor, Valerie Wyatt, for her
sense of humour, encouraging words and
fine editing skills.

PAPER is a master of disguise. It can be thin enough to see through and thick enough to sit on. It can be folded into a carton, scrunched into a ball or made into tissues gentle enough for a baby's bottom. It can be corrugated or smooth, coloured or bleached, waterproof or absorbent, pliable or rigid, fireproof or flammable. Most amazingly, every kind of paper is made the same way.

When you read *The Amazing Paper Book* you'll:
- meet some paper heroes and discover some paper legends
- learn how to make your own paper, pen and ink and write invisible messages
- follow the discovery of paper from ancient China to North America
- mystify your friends with tricky paper puzzlers
- and stun your family by cooking dinner in an envelope!

If you come across a paper-making word that you don't understand, check the glossary at the back of the book.

Paper makes the world go round

As your alarm clock buzzes, you huddle under your blankets and dream of spending the day in bed. There's a math test today.

You're no whiz at math but you have a wonderful imagination. In your hazy morning dozing, you dream up a fairy godmother who can grant your every whim. You imagine her waving a wand and making the math tests fly off the teacher's desk and out the window. But the clock ticks and there's no time for dreams. As you struggle out of bed, you have an eerie feeling that you are being watched. Out of the corner of your eye, you see the real thing — a fairy godmother complete with wand and pink tutu! You blink. She's still there. You rub your eyes. She smiles. And then she whips her wand through the air and shouts: "Done! The papers are gone."

You can't believe this is happening. There won't be a math test after all. Then you realize your fairy godmother has gone too far. Everywhere you look, paper is flying through the windows and out the doors. Your fairy godmother has made *all* the paper disappear.

"Yo! Fairy godmother," you shout. But your fairy godmother has gone the way of the paper — out the window.

This isn't so bad, you think to yourself. Who needs paper anyway?

You, for one. The bathroom isn't the same without paper. There are no labels on the tubes and bottles — you can't tell the toothpaste from the hair gel. There's no Kleenex, and you guessed it: there's no toilet paper. (Before the invention of toilet paper people used old catalogues and newspapers. Before that, they used rags, moss and grass.) "Fairy godmother," you scream. "Where are you when I need you?"

You go to the kitchen for some cereal. Uh, oh — cereal boxes are made of paper. You forget about breakfast and start making lunch. Uh, oh — no waxed paper for the sandwiches, no napkins and no brown bags. Lunch might be a bit of a mess.

As you head out the door, you realize that you have no homework to show, no papers or workbooks. Sounds great? Think again. You have to do all your learning by listening and memorizing.

It doesn't take long before you're bellowing for your fairy godmother. A math quiz is less of a problem than living in a world without paper.

Why we need paper

Paper is everywhere — around your pizza, at home, at school and even in hospital operating rooms. But have you ever wondered why people invented paper? There's a one-word answer: writing.

Writing was invented long before paper. At first people wrote on clay tablets. Imagine lugging clay tablets around, and think how tough it must have been to correct a mistake. Later, people wrote on parchment and vellum made from animal skin. If you wanted to write a letter in those days, you had to kill a sheep or calf, skin it, soften the skin with lime and then pound it with a rock. Because of these difficulties, parchment and vellum were as precious as gold and jewels. Only a handful of privileged people — mostly priests — learned to read and write.

When paper was invented, the world changed. Paper was easy to make from old cloth or reeds. It was also cheap to make, so it could be mass-produced for the regular folks, not just the high priests.

One thing led to another. Pens and ink were invented. The printing press was invented. (Much to the relief of monks who slaved for years to copy books by hand.) Books became commonplace.

More and more people learned to read. But as more people demanded books, it became harder and harder to find the cloth needed to make the paper. Clever inventors came up with a way to turn trees into paper instead. This "pulp paper," the kind you use today, started a paper revolution. Pulp made from crushed-up trees could be turned into boxes, napkins, bathroom tissue...even pianos. Soon paper took over from cloth because it was so cheap it could be thrown out after just one use.

You can almost trace the entire history of human beings by following the inventions that led to the discovery of paper...and paper products.

Before there was paper...

The ancient Egyptians discovered that a common reed, papyrus, growing alongside the Nile River could be made into a durable, light, flat writing surface. The Egyptians cut the long papyrus reeds into thin strips and put them side by side. Another layer of papyrus strips was criss-crossed on top to make what looked like a paper mat. Next, water was poured onto the mat. Then the Egyptians spent hours rubbing the mat with a stone until it was smooth. Papyrus was popular, but many people — especially Europeans — preferred parchment. It was made from the skins of kids (baby goats) and lambs. Even softer writing material called vellum was made from the skin of calves. The animal skins were made soft, pliable and smooth by coating them with a mixture of chalk and lime paste and leaving them in the sun to dry. Once dried, the animal skins were rubbed with a stone to make them smooth enough for writing.

Make your own pen...

Before the days of ball-point pens, kids wrote with quill pens. You can make one yourself. Search your backyard, woods or beach in the summer when the birds are moulting. Chances are you'll find a feather. The hollow stock is called the quill. Feathers from large birds such as geese make the best pens.

You'll need:
a feather
a sharp knife
ink
blotting paper or paper towel

1. Pluck some of the feathery part off the thick end of the quill so you can hold it.

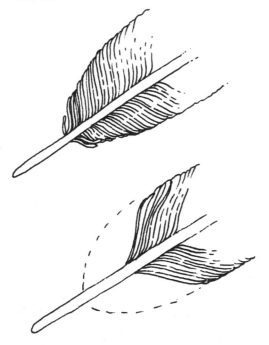

2. Cut the quill end at a slight angle, then cut the end of the quill like this:

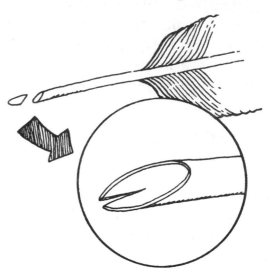

3. Dip the pen into some ink and write. Keep a blotter or paper towel handy because you might blob until you get the hang of it.

...and ink

Try making some berry ink like your pioneer ancestors. You could probably write with the berry juice alone but adding vinegar helps keep the rich colour and salt stops the juice from going mouldy.

You'll need:
a strainer
a mixing bowl
a spoon
a small jar with tight fitting lid

125 mL of blueberries	½ cup
2 mL vinegar	½ tsp
2 mL salt	½ tsp

1. Hold the strainer over the bowl.
2. Pour the blueberries into the strainer and crush the berries with the spoon.
3. Keep crushing the berries until all the juice has squished into the bowl. Throw away the crushed blueberry pulp.
4. Add the vinegar and salt to the berry juice.
5. Pour the ink into the jar and cover until ready to use.

You can make other kinds of ink from nut shells and tree bark. (Never skin bark from a tree: use fallen-off bark.)

You'll need:
paper towels
a hammer
a small saucepan
a small jar with tight fitting lid

250 mL nut shells (try peanuts, hazel-nuts, chestnuts or even pieces of bark)	1 cup
250 mL water	1 cup
2 mL salt	½ tsp
2 mL vinegar	½ tsp

1. Wrap the nut shells in a piece of paper towel.
2. Hammer the shells into little pieces.
3. Put the water and crushed shells into a saucepan. Heat until the water is boiling. Turn the stove to low and cook for about one hour.
4. Take the pot off the stove and let the ink cool.
5. Add the salt and vinegar to the ink.
6. Store in the jar with the lid closed until ready to use.

Write on!

The next time you pick up a pen or pencil, think of the ancient Sumerians who first invented writing in the Middle East more than 5000 years ago. They had a rule that part of everything each family owned must be given to the priests in the temple. But remember — writing hadn't been invented yet. There was no way of marking personal belongings and no way to keep records of who had given what.

So, the priests worked out a system. Each family was assigned a symbol — perhaps a pitchfork or a goose egg — that was engraved on a small cylinder of stone. Each family rolled its seal over a piece of soft clay, let it dry and then used leather thongs to attach these "necklaces" to their animals or household goods. That cleared up the problem of what belonged to whom. But since numbers hadn't been invented, there was no way of keeping track of how much each family owed. The priests came up with another bright idea: they drew pictures of all the different goods owned by the families — wheat, cows, lambs and so on — and carved a line under each thing given to the temple.

The priests realized that symbols could also represent ideas. For instance, a drawing of a shaft of wheat could represent wheat or the idea of plenty. These idea pictures are called ideographs.

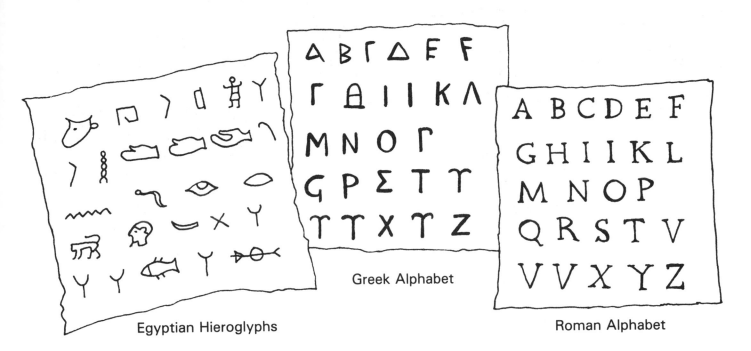

Egyptian Hieroglyphs

Greek Alphabet

Roman Alphabet

Then the priests made an amazing discovery. If they gave a symbol for each sound, they could make many new words from a few basic symbols. That discovery was the beginning of the writing system we use today — the phonetic alphabet. The Sumerians used 500 symbols — triangles, squiggles and lines — for syllables and vowels and carved them into soft clay with pens made from reeds.

As writing spread through the Middle East it took different forms. The Egyptians made an alphabet of animal and people drawings called hieroglyphs. They filled hollow reeds with ink made from a mixture of soot and water and charcoal — the first fountain pens — and drew on woven papyrus reeds.

Around 1500 B.C., the Chinese developed their own written language — a combination of ideographs and phonetic symbols. There were thousands of these symbols. The Chinese made ink, but instead of drawing on paper, they drew onto silk cloths with fine brushes made of camel hair.

The written language has gone through many changes around the world. Our alphabet with 26 symbols (letters) was adapted from the Middle-Eastern alphabet by the Greeks and the Romans around 1000 B.C.

Getting from A to B (alphabet to book)

In ancient times most people didn't learn to read or write. Why not? Reading wasn't easy. Papyrus, parchment and vellum were so precious that words were writtentogetherlike thiswithoutanyspacespunctuationmarksorevenpagenumbers. Parchment pages were glued together into scrolls hundreds of metres (yards) long. Imagine trying to find just one sentence in the middle of a thick roll!

Thousands of European monks spent their lives painstakingly copying ancient scrolls to preserve the knowledge they contained. There had to be a way of making thousands of copies of books cheaply and quickly so that everyone could read them.

The Chinese had the answer. It was called block printing, and the Chinese had been doing it since the T'ang Dynasty in 618. One emperor is said to have had 40 000 printed scrolls in his library! The Chinese made an ink by mixing the soot from oil lamps with oil or water. They carefully carved pictures and words into wooden blocks and covered them with ink. The printers then laid a sheet of paper or silk on the block, and rubbed it with a brush — presto, a printed page. There was only one problem with block printing — once a block was carved it could never be changed.

By the eleventh century, the Chinese were experimenting with a new type of printing called "movable type." A man named Ch'ing-li Pi Sheng made a clay mould of every character in the Chinese alphabet. Every time he wanted to print a new page, Sheng moved the characters to make new words and sentences. But even that had its problems. There were 30 000 characters in the Chinese alphabet then and nobody could find the right characters when they needed them. It was almost as bad as finding one grain of sugar in a shaker-full of salt. Needless to say, the Chinese went back to block printing.

Thousands of individual letters were arranged into words, sentences and paragraphs. These were covered with ink then put on the printing press.

By turning a handle the printer pressed a piece of paper against the inked letters.

Metal letters were made backwards so that they would print the right way.

In 1450 a German silversmith named Johann Gutenberg re-invented the idea of movable type. He built a printing press using letters moulded out of metal. Gutenberg was luckier than the Chinese; he had only 26 letters to worry about. His printing press was so sophisticated that his 200 copies of the Bible published in 1456 are thought to be some of the finest examples of publishing ever.

The buck starts here

Before there was paper money, people exchanged what they had for what they needed. It was complicated and difficult when large exchanges had to be made. Put yourself in the shoes of the leaders of twelfth-century China. They lost a battle to warring nomads who wanted a pay-off. What could they possibly give? Their crops had been destroyed in battle and there was a shortage of precious metals and jewels. They did what you would do in the same boat — they gave an I.O.U. The clever Chinese printed notes made from perfumed silk paper promising silver or gold. It was the first paper money.

The explorer Marco Polo was astonished to find people trading with mere paper instead of with gold, silver and rubies. He called the exchange of paper a mysterious alchemy: people seemed to turn paper into gold.

Today, only governments can print money and they have to back it up

with real gold bars stored in vaults. When you write a cheque, you are making a promise that *you* have enough money in your bank account to pay up.

Making money

The first-ever cheque was written by Nicholas Vanacker in London, England, on April 22, 1659, for a total of 10 British pounds. The same cheque sold at an auction in 1976 for 1300 British pounds!

16

You might think that paper would burn to a crisp in an oven. (Actually it would burn if the temperature were more than 230°C [450°F].) But at medium oven temperatures you can cook delicious dinners in an envelope made of a special cooking paper called parchment paper. The best part about a parchment paper pouch (try saying that with a mouthful!) is opening it once it's cooked. All the aromas that were locked inside come whooshing out.

This recipe is for Chinese chicken in a pouch but you could experiment with fish for a change. Make each serving individually. This recipe serves one.

You'll need:
a cookie sheet
a small mixing bowl
a small knife
a stirring spoon

5 mL soya sauce	1 tsp
5 mL honey	1 tsp
5 mL vegetable oil	1 tsp

1 chopped green onion (white and
    green parts)
a handful of cashews or shelled peanuts
1 chicken breast with the skin off and
    the bone removed (you can buy
    chicken breasts this way at the store)
1 large sheet of parchment paper

1. Turn on the oven to 160°C (325°F).
2. Mix the soya sauce, honey, vegetable oil, chopped green onion and nuts in a bowl.

3. Put the chicken breast in the middle of the parchment paper and pour all the ingredients from the bowl over the chicken.
4. Take one edge of the parchment paper and fold it over the chicken until it meets the far edge. Crimp the edges together until you have made a "closed envelope." Make sure the package is tightly sealed.

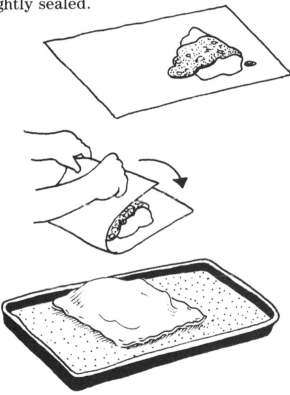

5. Put the envelope on the cookie sheet and bake for 30 minutes.
6. Put the envelope on a plate and serve. You don't eat the paper! Undo your pouch and enjoy. Great with a bowl of rice, some chopsticks and your favourite salad.

Modern paper inventions

Quick! Name three paper inventions you couldn't manage without. Right! Toilet paper, Kleenex and brown paper bags.

Wipe it!

The first toilet paper was folded up into sheets and sold in packages of 500 for 50 cents. Sounds like a bargain, but the idea bombed in 1857 for inventor Joseph Gayetty of New York. People couldn't understand why they should pay good money for toilet paper when there was lots of paper such as old catalogues and newspapers around.

Even the first rolls of toilet paper, invented in England two years later, didn't sell. The Victorian prudes didn't want to hear about such private matters. But in America, times were changing. Indoor plumbing was the rage. Two enterprising Americans, the Scott brothers, who were already selling paper napkins, branched into selling small rolls of perforated toilet paper. They said it was "soft as old linen" and made a fortune.

Blow it!

At least the Scott brothers knew their product and how to advertise it. The inventors of Kleenex had no idea they had designed the perfect throw-away handkerchief.

During World War I, the Kimberly-Clark company made a substitute for cotton out of paper. It was used as bandages on the battlefields. After the war, the company tried to sell its tissue as a substitute for face-cloths. But people began blowing their noses with it instead.

Bag it!

Until 1883, brown paper bags had V-shaped bottoms and were pasted together by hand. They didn't hold much and you had to steady them with one hand and fill them with the other. Fortunately, Charles Stilwell invented the first machine to make flat-bottomed paper bags with pleated sides.

Wear it!

Years ago it would have been unthinkable to put babies in anything but the softest cloth diapers. Today there is hardly a baby who isn't swaddled in layers of absorbent paper.

Wearing paper has caught on with older folks too. Surgeons and nurses wear paper gowns, caps and even booties in the operating room because paper can be sterilized before use and destroyed after use. Someone even came up with paper underwear and — hold onto your (paper) hat — even bathing-suits.

Paper firsts

Julius Caesar started the **first newspaper**. It featured details of criminal trials, births, deaths, marriages and events at the Circus Maximus and Coliseum. It was published daily and posted on walls so that everyone could read it. There was only one problem: Julius Caesar made the decisions about all the news that was fit to print. You can bet the paper never suggested that Julius be thrown to the lions!

The Dutch were the first to publish a newspaper with social and political news from around the world, in 1605.

Before photocopying was invented, people made duplicate copies with carbon paper. The **first carbon paper** was made in 1806 by Ralph Wedgewood of London, England, who saturated thin paper with ink and let it dry between sheets of blotting paper.

The **first Christmas card** was privately designed and produced in England for Sir Henry Cole who sent it to all his friends in 1843. The idea caught on and by 1880, there were so many Christmas cards that the British post office developed the slogan "Post Early for Christmas!"

20

The **first comic strip** was a Sunday colour supplement of the *New York Journal* on October 24, 1897. It featured "The Yellow Kid" who had a bald head and floppy ears.

Cardboard had been around since 1700 but nobody was quite sure what to do with it. Robert Gair of Brooklyn, New York, first invented a machine that could cut and crease cardboard to make the **first cartons**. But it took a biscuit company to make cartons a success.

In 1899, the National Biscuit Company introduced a new product — a soda cracker called "Uneeda Biscuit." They packaged the crackers in cardboard cartons to stop the biscuits from going stale. Around each carton was a printed wrapper suggesting that the carton could be used for kids' lunch boxes after the crackers were gone.

The cardboard carton was a hit. Soon there were milk cartons, cereal boxes (the first to print right on the box instead of on a wrapper) and juice boxes. Today North Americans use almost half a million cardboard packages a day.

Neat thing to do with paper #2: **Make a pop-up card**

All you need is scissors, a pencil and a ruler and glue to turn two pieces of paper into a talking pop-up card.

1. Take two pieces of paper, each 21.5 cm x 28 cm (8½ inches x 11 inches). Fold each paper in half. Put one aside.

2. On the other, put a dot in approximately the centre of the folded edge.

3. Draw a 5 cm (2 inch) line from the dot towards the outer edge.

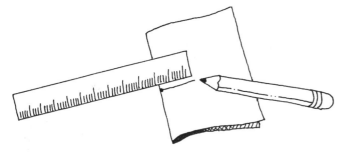

4. Starting at the folded edge, cut on the line.

5. Fold back the flaps to form two triangles.

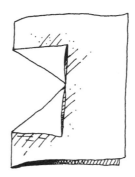

6. Open up the flaps again. Open the whole page.

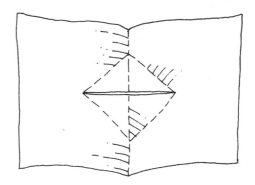

7. Now comes the tricky part! Hold your paper, so that it looks like a tent. Put your finger on the top triangle and push down. Pinch the two folded edges of the top triangle, so that the triangle is pushed through to the other side of the paper.

8. Put your finger on the bottom triangle and do the same thing. The top and bottom triangles will now be pushed out to form a mouth inside the card. When you open and close your card, the mouth will look like it is talking. When your card is closed, it will look like this:

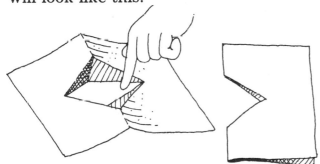

9. Draw a monster, a person or an animal around your mouth.

10. Glue the inside and outside cards together. *Do not apply glue in the area of the pop-up mouth.* You now have a cover for your card.

Other Ideas

1. Draw a jagged line, instead of a straight line, for the talking mouth. Your figure will now have teeth.

2. Draw a head and body around the mouth. Make sure the body is wider than the head, so that your figure can stand.

Neat thing to do with paper #3: **Make a string block print**

You can make wonderful designs for pictures or wrapping paper by using the ancient method of block printing.

You'll need:
string
3 small blocks of wood
3 different colours of paint
3 foil pie plates
paper (brown wrapping paper, white paper or even tissue paper)

1. Wrap a piece of string around a block of wood a couple of times.
2. Wrap each of the three blocks with string. Make sure that you don't wrap string on top of string.

3. Pour one colour of paint in each of the three pie plates.

4. Make your first string block print by dipping a block into one of the colours and pressing it firmly down on a piece of paper. Repeat the design as often as you like.
5. Repeat using other colours.

The million prayers

The Empress Koken of Japan was first to print with copper, not wooden, blocks. In the year 763 she ordered that one million good luck charms (dharani) be printed. Each charm was 25 lines long and was enshrined in a miniature, three-storey pagoda. It took 100 printers seven years to finish the job!

Koken was terrified of a smallpox epidemic and offered the dharani to drive out disease demons. Her ploy didn't work. The Empress died of smallpox in 770, the same year that her million charms were finished.

The man who invented paper

Some archeologists believe that a Chinese man named Ts'ai Lun invented paper. Other experts think it is more likely that Ts'ai's ancestors had been making a simple version of paper for generations and that he came up with a new, improved version.

Amazingly, the way we make paper today is based on the same principles used by Ts'ai Lun more than 2000 years ago. Ts'ai threw old rags, torn up bits of fishing net, and hemp rope into a vat of boiling water and wood ash. Then he ground this mixture with a mortar and pestle until it made a pulpy mass like porridge. He poured the pulp onto a cloth screen sieve and let all the water drip out. The fibres stuck together and dried in the sun. What was left could be lifted in one piece. It was paper!

To convince people to use his new invention, Ts'ai came up with an elaborate plan. He hid away and let everyone believe he had died. His business partners staged a funeral. His partners told the crowd of mourners that Ts'ai had one last wish — that they burn paper over his grave. They said Ts'ai believed burnt paper had the power to give long and everlasting life. The villagers were sceptical but dutifully burned bits of paper until the grave was covered with ash. Then Ts'ai's friends dug up the body. He was alive!

His magical secret wasn't burnt paper. He had been buried alive and managed to breathe through a thin, hollow bamboo tube that snaked from the coffin through the ground to the air above. But the villagers didn't see through the scam and clamoured for their own paper charms to give them everlasting life.

Ts'ai Lun was too devious for his own good. After the great success with paper, he was honoured by the royal court and given a high position. Later, he turned against the ruler and was caught in a palace scandal. Ts'ai did what was considered honourable: he swallowed a vial of deadly poison.

Old paper

Two Chinese professors were exploring the ruins of a watch-tower in the Chinese mountains of Bayan-Bogdo when they discovered a crumpled, thick, rough ball of paper decorated with 12 Chinese characters. They took it for tests and discovered it was the oldest piece of paper ever discovered. It was buried around 109 A.D.

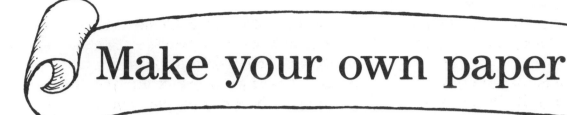

Make your own paper

You can make paper almost the same way the Chinese did thousands of years ago.

You'll need:
5 sheets of clean white paper
hot water
2 picture frames the same size
a piece of fine mesh like the kind used for screens cut slightly larger than the frames
a stapler and staples
a large bowl
a blender
warm water
food colouring (optional)
a deep basin half-filled with warm water
two old towels or blankets
J-cloths
spray starch
a strainer

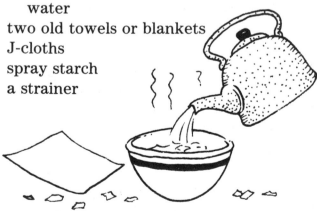

1. Tear the paper into pieces about 2 cm (1 inch) square and mix them with hot water in the bowl. Let the mixture soak for 30 minutes.

2. Remove the glass from the picture frames. Put one frame aside. It will be your deckle.
3. Make a mould by stapling mesh all around the outside of the other frame.

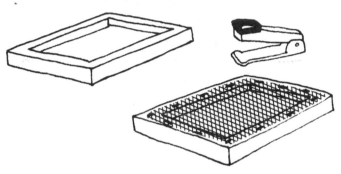

4. Put the mould, screen side down, on a table. Put the deckle on top. Hold the mould and deckle together.

5. Make the pulp this way: pour the warm water into the blender. Scoop a handful of the soaked paper into the blender. Blend at medium speed until you can't see any bits of paper. It should look like a soupy mush. If you want coloured paper, add a few drops of food colouring.

6. Pour the pulp into the basin half-filled with water. This should make a thin paper. If you want a thicker paper, make some more pulp in your blender and add it to the basin. You may have to experiment to get just the thickness you want.

7. Hold the mould and deckle firmly in your hands. In one smooth motion, dip your mould and deckle in and out of the pulp. As you do this you'll catch the pulp on the screen. Hold the mould and deckle over the basin and gently shake it forward and backward and then from side to side. Most of the water will flow through the mesh screen and you'll be left with a matted pulp on the mould.

8. Put the mould and deckle aside for a moment. Lay the towel or blanket on a counter top or table. Wet a J-cloth with water and put it on top of the towel. Keep your second towel handy.

9. Carefully lift the deckle off the mould. In one smooth motion flip the mould upside down onto the wet J-cloth. Using your fingers, rub the mesh lightly to press out any extra water.

10. Gently and slowly lift the screen. The paper will stick to the J-cloth. Let it dry. (You can speed up the drying by covering the paper with a towel and ironing.)

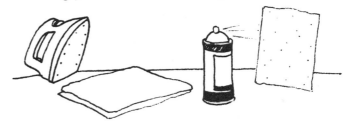

11. Spray the paper with starch.

12. Don't throw the pulp mixture down the drain. It could gum up your sink. Instead, strain the pulp and store it in a plastic bag in your freezer. Use it again next time.

Pulp is made from the cellulose fibres found in plants; you can experiment by making paper with different plant fibres. When you make the pulp, try adding one of these items to the paper pieces and water mixture: left-over cooked broccoli or carrots, straw, grass, onion skins or even shredded string. One thing that *doesn't* make good home-made paper is cotton balls!

Hand-made paper

Early papermakers made paper by hand much the same way you've just done. First they would add water to cotton and linen rags and grind them up. But instead of a blender, they did the grinding by hand, with a mortar and pestle. They would keep adding water and grind and pound until the rags had broken down into a mush. This mush was called pulp. Then they would strain the water out of the pulp much the same way you did, and press out the last of the moisture. It took five men a whole day to make 800 sheets of paper. And it was hard work.

Papermakers had a terrible life. They worked 12 hours a day bending over steaming vats in dark, wet rooms. In those days you could tell a man was a papermaker by the way he looked; papermakers had hunched backs and brilliant red skin on their faces and arms from the hot steam.

Secret Chinese messages

Chinese writing is very complex, and it takes a long time to master the direction and thickness of the strokes. But you can learn some of the basic symbols. Use a brush and ink for the best results.

The best thing about Chinese writing is that sometimes two characters can be combined to make a new meaning. For instance, if you take the character for heaven and the character for person, you have a symbol that means angel. Here are some other examples:

below + mountain = climb down the mountain

sun + month = bright

What words might you get when you combine the characters for:

mountain + water

fire + mountain

Chinese sentences are structured the same way as English sentences — the subject is first, the verb is second and the object is last. All adjectives come before the noun they modify. There are no plural nouns in Chinese writing. Can you make this sentence in Chinese characters?

One day two people climb down the mountain.

Answers on page 76.

人 — person

下 — below

山 — mountain

有 — have, possess, exist, there is

日 — day, sun

月 — month

水 — water

一 — one

二 — two

三 — three

女 — woman

火 — fire

Nature's papermakers

If you look at a piece of wasp nest and a sheet of paper under a microscope, it's almost impossible to tell the difference. That's because wasps and people make paper in almost the same way — by chewing up wood into a pulp.

The queen wasp starts the process. She is the only survivor in a wasp nest after the cold winter. Few queens start a new family in an old nest. Instead the queen finds a new spot for a nest. Some types of paper wasps make nests high in a tree or under the eaves of a building; others nest underground.

To start the nest, the queen chews up fibres from old wood or paper trash, mixing them with her saliva until the material is pulpy. She drinks muddy water and regurgitates it at the nest to glue the paper fibres together.

The wasp up close

Only one family of wasps — paper wasps — make paper nests. Paper wasps are easy to recognize because they're thin and black or brown with yellow or orange stripes on their abdomens. They have a stinger to protect themselves and sharp mandibles (jaws) to scrape rotten wood from trees or houses. And in the fall after they've finished the hard work of feeding the larvae and building the nest they like to bother you and eat your food!

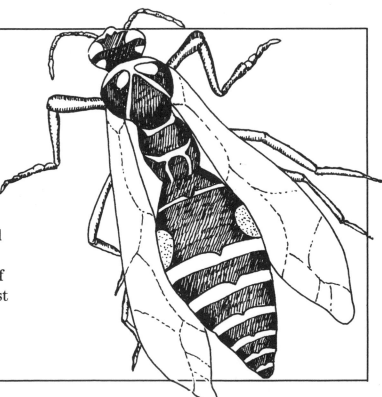

The queen makes a long stalk with a bell-shaped canopy, then adds a small layer of round paper rooms called cells and lays an egg in each one. As she keeps building rooms, the sides get squished into an octagonal shape. She covers each layer of cells with a paper umbrella. After the eggs hatch, she feeds her grubs (larvae) and keeps up the hard work of building and laying eggs.

When the wasp grubs are fully grown, they change into pupae, much as caterpillars change inside cocoons. The queen makes a silk cover over each pupa. Inside, the pupae change into female wasps called workers that gnaw their way out of their cells.

Everyone gets busy. By now the paper umbrella over the cells is the shape and size of a football with a small opening at the bottom. The queen has done her hardest work: now she only lays eggs. The workers build cells, get food for her majesty and feed the new larvae. By the end of the summer, a single wasp nest can have 12 000 cells.

Late in the fall, some of the eggs develop as new queens. These new queens will build nests for themselves the next spring.

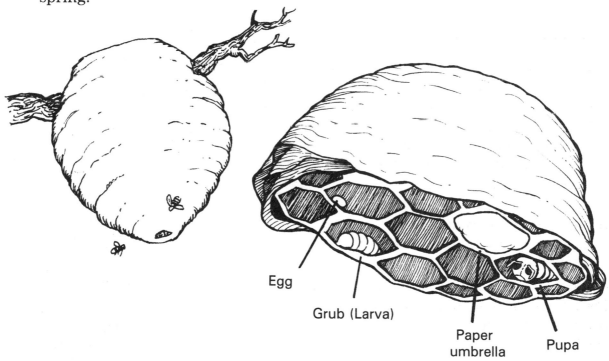

Egg

Grub (Larva)

Paper umbrella

Pupa

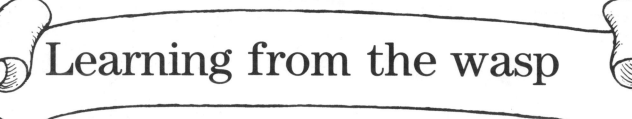

Learning from the wasp

By the beginning of the nineteenth century papermakers started running out of rags to make paper.

Papermakers needed a substitute for rags. French scientist René de Réaumur looked to nature for the answer. He studied the paper wasp and announced that he had found a way to make paper entirely from wood fibres. That was in November 1719, but nothing was done about Réaumur's far-sighted idea for more than a century.

In 1840 a German weaver named Friedrich Keller invented a machine that could grind a stick of wood into fibres. In 1841 two Englishmen, Burgess and Watt, discovered another way of

The search for rags

In the middle of the rag shortage, two enterprising Americans heard that the Egyptian railroads were using the linen wrappings from mummies to fuel their trains. If the Egyptians could use the old linens, why not the paper industry? So they started importing the mummies and stripping off the fine linen to make pulp. There could be up to 18 kg (40 pounds) of linen around a princess. (The Egyptians also mummified cats, cows and crocodiles.)

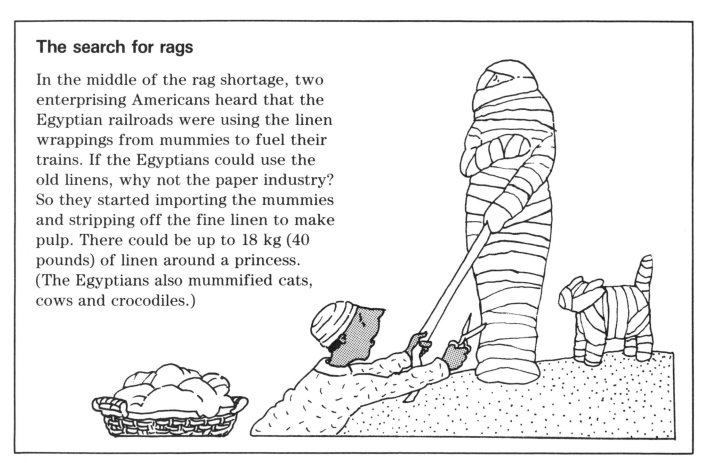

breaking wood into fibres. They boiled wood chips in a
chemical brew called caustic alkali. And in 1865, American
Benjamin Tilghman made an even stronger fibre by cooking
wood chips in a different chemical, sodium sulphite.

These inventors pointed to the way of the future. By the
time of Canada's Confederation in 1867, most of the mills in
North America and Europe used wood pulp instead of rags to
make paper. Now all they needed were mill sites with water
for power, good shipping routes and a close supply of timber.
The North American wilderness had it all.

Paper puzzlers

If you think of paper as pretty ordinary stuff, think again. Paper can be puzzling, perplexing and downright problematic. Here are some paper puzzlers to tease your brain. Take your time, because there are some tricks here.

Keeping dry

How can you drop a paper napkin in water and keep it dry?

You'll need:
a paper napkin or piece of paper towel
a drinking glass
a clear bowl or container
water

1. Stuff the paper napkin tightly into the bottom of the glass.
2. Fill the bowl with water.
3. Turn the glass upside down and plunge it into the water. Make sure you hold it straight down. Hold it there for a while.

4. Remove the glass. Pull out the napkin. Why is it dry?

How does it work?
Although the glass looks empty to you, it's full — of air! The air keeps the water from touching the paper. Try the trick again, only this time tilt the glass slightly. Why do you think the napkin gets wet?

Magic hugging paper clips

Bet you can't make two paper clips hug each other.

You'll need:
a paper dollar bill
2 paper clips

1. Fold the paper bill like this:

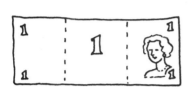 

2. Attach the paper clips exactly like this:

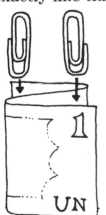 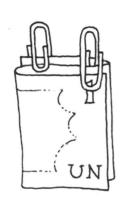

3. Hold the ends of the bill, make sure no one is in the line of fire, and snap the ends of the bill as if it were a Christmas cracker. Presto — you'll have two linked paper clips.

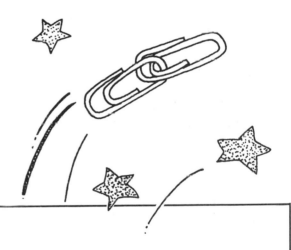

Unfolding a mystery

Can you fold a piece of paper — any paper — ten times?

You'll need:
3 pieces of paper of different textures and sizes (try newspaper, notepaper, a greeting card)

1. Try to fold each piece of paper in half and half again.

2. Keep on folding. See if you can get past fold number nine.

Why doesn't it work?
Each time you fold the paper you create more layers. By the time you have folded the paper nine times you have 128 layers of paper. That's too thick for anyone to fold!

Paper Samson

If you've ever been bothered by a bully who claims to be bigger and stronger than all the kids, here's a challenge that should bring the bully down to size!

You'll need:
five double sheets of newspaper
a wooden ruler
a table

1. Spread the newspapers on the table.
2. Put the ruler under the newspapers, a few inches from the fold, so that about half of it extends over the table edge.

3. Try to lift the newspapers off by pounding on the ruler.

4. Get the bully to try. No matter how strong he is, he won't be able to lift the newspapers.

How does it work?
There's a lot of air pressing down on the newspapers — 103 kPa (15 pounds on every square inch)! No wonder the bully can't lift the newspapers. If he tries too hard, he might even break the ruler.

Making cubes

If you unglued a square box, you'd find one piece of cardboard folded into six equal squares.

Suppose you started with six squares of paper. How many ways could you arrange them and still get a cube.

Answer on page 76.

You'll need:
6 equal-sized square pieces of
    cardboard or paper
glue or tape

1. Arrange the squares into different shapes.
2. Glue or tape the edges together.
3. Fold into a cube, if possible.
4. Make diagrams of the arrangements that could be folded into cubes and count them.

Why do paper cuts hurt so much?

You know that whenever you cut yourself with a knife or razor the nerve endings in your skin tell your brain that you have PAIN! But how can an innocent piece of paper cause so much agony?

The answer lies in the strength of paper and pressure. Paper is strong because of its interwoven fibres. When you strike your finger with a piece of paper, the paper doesn't curl up — it meets your fingertip head on.

You get paper cuts when you push the edge of a piece of paper suddenly and vigorously against your skin. Since you are using a lot of force over a small area (the thin edge of the paper) you are creating pressure. Your skin is no match for all that pressure — the paper slices through your skin. The thinner the paper, the more chances for a paper cut.

A weighty question

Can you support a thick book on the edge of a single sheet of paper?

You'll need:
typing paper
tape
a book

1. Fold and/or tape single sheets of paper into different shapes. Can you come up with a shape that supports a book?
Amazingly, a cylinder, triangle or star shape will work. Even paper folded into accordion pleats will support a book.

Why does it work?
If you tried to support a book on the thin edge of a piece of paper, the paper would crush and the book would topple. That's because all the weight of the book would be concentrated on a small surface area. By changing the shape of the paper into a cylinder, star or triangle you are increasing the surface area of the paper. The weight of the book can be distributed over a greater surface area. Surprise. One piece of paper can support *hundreds* of pieces of paper!

Building a better bridge

Try building paper bridges. Challenge your friends to see who can build the strongest bridge. Although you will all be given the same building materials, you do not need to use them all to build a strong bridge.

You'll need:
2 paper cups and 2 pieces of paper for each builder
tape
pennies for strength testing

1. Each builder is given two paper cups, two pieces of paper and tape.
2. The builders are allowed to fold, bend or tape their materials.
3. When the bridges are constructed, test the strength of each bridge by piling pennies in the centre of each bridge. The bridge that supports the most money is the strongest.

Answer on page 76.

In Japan, there is an ancient legend that the crane lives for a thousand years and that any sick person who folds 1000 paper cranes will be granted a wish to be healthy again. A brave 11-year-old girl named Sadako Sasaki desperately wanted to believe that story.

Many years after the Americans ended World War II by dropping an atomic bomb on the Japanese city of Hiroshima, Sadako became ill with leukemia — a cancer that can be caused by the radiation released from the bomb. She was weak, but every day she folded paper cranes. On the day she died, October 25, 1955, she had a flock of 644 cranes to flutter from the ceiling of her hospital room.

Sadako's schoolmates were heart-broken. They folded 356 cranes so that Sadako could be buried with a thousand cranes. Some friends thought that there should be a monument to Sadako and all the children who were killed by the atom bomb. School children all over Japan collected coins until there was enough money to build a monument. Today in the centre of the Hiroshima Peace Park, there is a statue of Sadako standing on top of a mountain holding a golden crane.

On Peace Day every August 6, people make thousands of paper cranes and leave them at the foot of Sadako's statue in the hope that no one will forget why a brave little girl died.

It is very difficult to make origami cranes, but you might start paper-folding by making this bird.

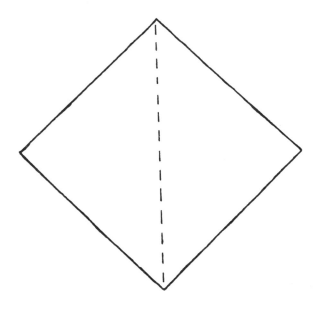

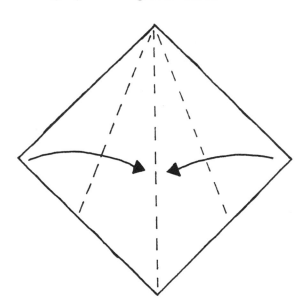

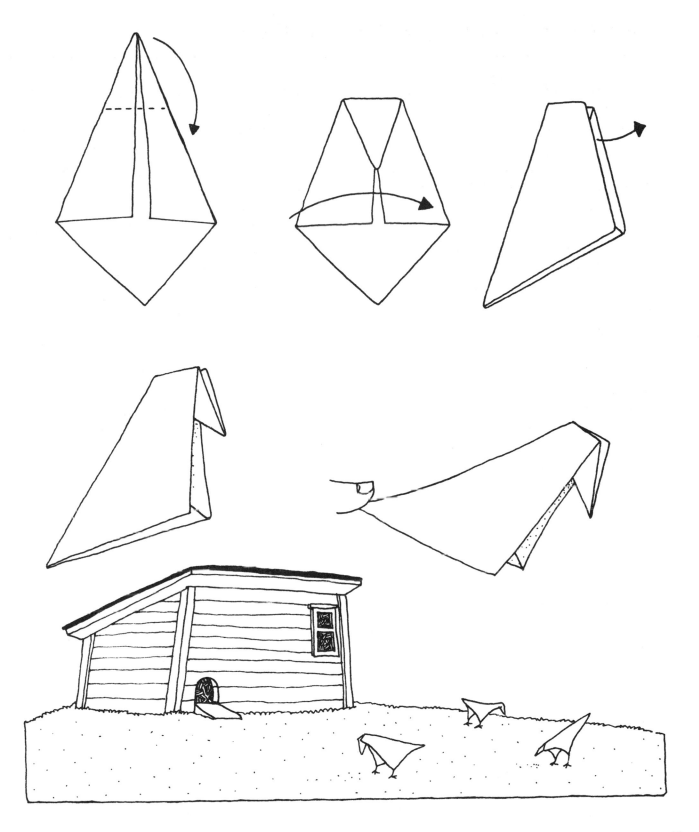

Pioneer loggers could make you shiver with stories about cutting tree trunks that were as wide as wagons or waking with their eyelashes frozen shut because the winter nights were so cold. They could tell you about forests so thick with black flies that men died of infections from the bites. Why would anyone take on a dirty, cold, dangerous and lonely job in the wilderness? For one reason — money. Most of the pioneers were farmers. They needed the money paid by the logging companies to keep their livestock and their families alive through the winter.

Life in the logging camps was rough. The loggers went into the woods in the fall, right after the harvest. Their first job was to build a one-room log cabin called a shanty. There was a hole in the roof for the smoke from the ever-burning campfire in the centre of the shanty. The beds were made of saplings covered with tar paper and pine boughs. Sometimes the men stuffed newspapers between their blankets for extra warmth. The wind would howl through the cracks in the shanty walls forcing most loggers to sleep in their coats and hats.

Loggers ate the same thing day after day — peas, beans, salt pork, bread, cheese, tea and molasses. Before vitamin pills were invented, many loggers suffered from scurvy because they had no Vitamin C from fruits and vegetables. In the good camps, the cooks served dried fruits and canned tomatoes to prevent this problem.

The foreman was the "bull of the camp." He knew every job to be done and kept the men working. One group of men — the choppers — felled the trees with saws and axes — and the roar of "Tiiiimmmmbbberrr!" echoed through the forest.

Once a tree was felled, it was cut into shorter logs that could be dragged out of the forest by horses or oxen to the side of a river or the roadside. The loggers made skid roads from short logs laid crosswise. They were icy and sometimes a

sleigh laden with logs stacked a storey high would gain
momentum and race down steep hills, crushing the men and
horses in its path.

Today logs are carted out of the forest by truck and turned
into lumber or paper at the mill. But in the early 1900s, much
of the work was done right in the forest. Wood to be used for
building was cut and smoothed by men called hewers. Twenty
hewed pieces of lumber were tied together into a square
"crib," and the cribs were lashed together into rafts. In
spring, the rafts were driven downriver by the men known as —
you guessed it — raftsmen.

The wood for the paper mills was driven in loose groups of
logs down the river. Logs could get stuck in bays, tight river
bends or get jammed up. River pushers and drivers had the
dangerous job of running along the moving logs, poking and
prodding them with sticks (or with dynamite) to loosen them

up. You may have seen a log-rolling contest — they're tame compared to the real thing on a river. Just one misplaced step could plunge a river driver into a raging, frigid river or make him slip between colliding logs.

Loggers on the west coast didn't have to fight the cold, but they had another problem — the trees themselves. They were enormous, with thick roots sticking up from the ground. Loggers had to climb up and over the roots to reach the trunk for chopping. And because they weren't standing on the ground, the loggers had to cut slits in the trunk and insert planks of wood like small diving boards around the tree. Six or more men could stand on one of these platforms and chop.

Since there was little farming and the climate was moderate, loggers on the west coast worked year-round. They greased their skid roads with whale oil so that the logs, pulled by teams of oxen called bulls, would slip along easily. Later, loggers used steam engines called donkeys to pull the trees out of the forest.

44

In the early days, the forests grew close to the coast. The trees could easily be skidded — pulled along the skid roads — to the coast and driven through the water to the mills. But as more and more forests were cut down, the loggers had to go higher into the mountains for trees. It was too dangerous and too expensive to build skid roads along the mountains.

To get the trees out, the loggers invented a "ski lift" for trees. A man called a high-rigger climbed the tallest tree in the area and cut off its top. Then he attached a system of cables and winches from the top of his tree tower to another tower some distance away. Logs were attached to the cable and pulled along by a steam engine. Today powerful diesel engines do the work instead of steam engines.

A heavy load

A felled softwood tree can weigh as much as 1 tonne (2200 pounds). That's the same as 14 full-grown men. Imagine pulling a whopper like that from the forest floor to a logging road. In eastern forests, huge machines called skidders drag the logs out with a power that even Paul Bunyan's ox Babe couldn't muster.

Tall tales of the lumberjacks

To pass the time, loggers played fiddle music and told some pretty tall tales. Jos Montferrand was a real-life logger in the early 1800s who roamed the Ottawa Valley and the area around Montreal. He was renowned for his athletic feats, his huge size and his talent as a riverman. Folks from San Francisco to Montreal spun stories about this hero of the lakes and woods. But many of the legends were forgotten when Montferrand died in 1884. Canadian storyteller Bernie Bedore salutes the memory of the real Montferrand by spinning tales of a mythical giant, Joe Mufferaw. One tall tale goes like this:

Joe Mufferaw was fishing on the shore of the Bonnechere River with his cook, Charlie Six-Hands. Well, the fish weren't biting so Joe hiked to his camp at Snow Boom, about 8 km (5 miles) away and was back in a few minutes with a steel cable,

a hook and a side of beef. He baited his line and waited.

After about an hour a big old catfish grabbed the line. Joe managed to hook his foot into a boom of logs. That old fish pulled Joe and the boom around the lake for three days and three nights.

On the third night, the fish saw a fire on the shore of the lake. Thinking it was the sun, it ploughed straight ahead. The catfish hit the shore and Joe went flying.

Folks figured it was the biggest fish ever landed — Joe sold the skin to the navy to make boats. The whiskers were made into masts. The eyeballs were encased in glass and Joe said they were made into the domes for a Maharajah's palace. A farmer used the ribs as rafters.

When Joe told his fish story, all folks could say was, "Yessiree, that was a big one."

Paul Bunyan was another legendary lumberjack. Some folks think he was bigger, stronger and faster than any logger before or since. He could outrun his own shadow and he combed his beard with a big old pine that he tore from the ground. When Paul was born in a sleepy town in Maine he weighed 90 kg (200 pounds). When he kicked he knocked over trees, and when he cried it sounded as if a hurricane were ripping through the woods.

One summer Paul went to visit another big man, Billy Pilgrim. Billy was digging the St. Lawrence River because there was nothing separating Canada and the United States and everybody got confused about which country was which. Billy and his pals had dug little more than a creek in three years. Paul boasted that he could dig the river in three weeks. Billy called the bluff and bet Paul a million dollars it couldn't be done.

Paul called for his workers — Johnnie Inkslinger the bookkeeper, Ole the big Swede, Brimstone Bill and Babe, Paul's pet blue ox. Paul never went anywhere without his cook, Hot Biscuit Slim and his assistant, Cream Puff Fatty. Paul could eat 200 pancakes, 22 hams, 65 sausages and a wagon-load of maple syrup for a light lunch.

They made a scooping shovel and attached it to Babe with a long rope. They dug every day and Babe hauled the dirt away to Vermont. Some people say the dirt is still there, only now it's called the Green Mountains of Vermont.

Billy Pilgrim tried to slow the work down by playing tricks. But Paul and his crew were just too smart and they finished in three weeks. Billy was a cheapskate and refused to pay up, so Paul picked up his shovel and started putting the dirt back in the river. Billy was worried. He offered to pay half the money he owed. But Paul kept on shovelling. Billy offered to pay two-thirds of the money he owed. Paul kept on shovelling. Finally, as Paul was throwing the one-thousandth shovelful of dirt, Billy handed over one million dollars.

Some people think you can still see all the shovel loads of dirt that Paul and his men threw into the St. Lawrence River — only now they're called the Thousand Islands.

Paul Bunyan's ring, actual size.

Logging today

In the olden days you could grab a saw, head into the woods and call yourself a lumberjack. Not anymore — now cutters wear protective clothing including hearing-protectors, eye-guards, helmets, leg guards, work boots, and they use powerful hand-held saws.

Today many forestry companies use machines that can do everything but clean your bedroom. Just one machine called a "tree harvester" can chop down a tree, cut off the top and big branches and stack the logs into piles in less than one minute flat!

Some people think these monster machines are hurting the land because their heavy wheels churn up or destroy the vital nutrient-packed top layers of soil. Other people say the wheels help break up the treetops and branches left on the ground for faster decomposition. This puts food back into the forest faster.

Ask a forester

A tree had to be cut down to make this book? So what, you might ask. There are a lot of trees — about half of Canada and a third of the land in the United States is forest. Trees are a renewable resource — they can be cut down, or even burned but eventually, new trees will take their place. So why worry? Nature is very slow, that's why. It takes at least 60 years and often 100 years for a harvested forest to grow back the way it was. Papermakers and other tree users are impatient; they want wood that's easy to find, easy to get out and perfect for paper or lumber.

So, instead of relying on nature, foresters have learned to "farm" forests. If you want to know how foresters farm, turn the page and ask Francine. She works for a paper company with a huge forest farm in British Columbia.

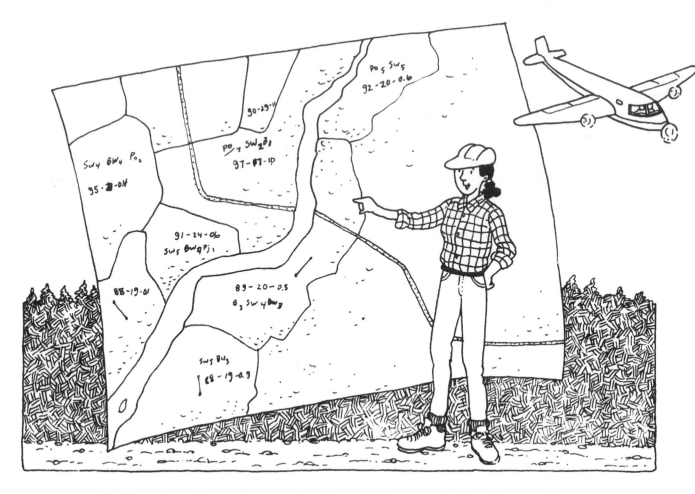

Q: Francine, how do you decide which trees in the forest to cut?

A: You might say we fly by the seat of our pants. We use airplanes with high-tech cameras to find out how many trees there are. Then we make predictions about how fast they'll grow and how many will die from bugs and fires. I draw a map showing exactly where to cut and when. Sometimes I wish I had a crystal ball because I have to look into the future and guess how many trees we'll need in 50 or 100 years!

Q: Do you plant the same kind of trees that you take out of the forest?

A: Sometimes. Natural forests have different kinds of trees growing together but we want only softwood trees to make paper. So we grow forests with one or two kinds of supertrees.

Insect friends and foes

Insects such as the spruce budworm that feed on the leaves and the buds of spruce and fir can devour entire forests. The bark beetle can destroy spruce and pine.

Fortunately, most bugs are good for forests. They make humus, the thin top layer of soil that gives life to the forest. Billions of ground insects break down dead leaves, rotted wood, plants and animal wastes, by constantly feeding, wiggling and squiggling through the debris. They churn up the soil with their constant movement so that it is spongy and roots can spread to pick up the nutrients such as nitrogen and potassium needed by growing plants. Flying insects fertilize plants and provide food for birds.

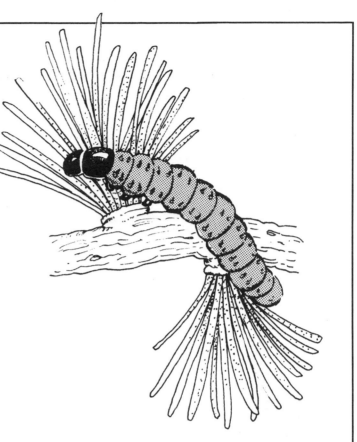

Q: Where do you get supertrees?
A: From the forest. During the summer we mark tall, healthy, fast-growing paper trees. In the winter we shoot off the tips of their branches with a rifle and graft these branch tips (scions) onto seedlings from a good tree. You might say we assemble supertrees out of bits and pieces that are already growing. Some day we might even be able to program these supertrees, with the help of genetic engineering. We might, for example, be able to reprogram trees that are water-guzzlers to grow in dryer places.

Q: How do you plant trees?
A: We're like farmers. Before we plant we have to get the land ready. First we stir up the duff — that's the layer of pine needles, leaves and other bits of nature's leftovers — with chains and jagged blades. Then we give the land a boost of nutrients or fertilizer. Sometimes we even set fire to the left-over branches and leaves to clear the land. The planting is the

easy part; we don't even have to bend over. The new plants come in little styrofoam containers called "plugs." We dig a hole with a tool called a dibble and pop the plug in.

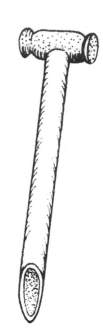

Q: How many do you plant?

A: It sounds like a lot — 1200 seedlings to a hectare (2.5 acres). But lots can go wrong. The seedlings could be planted improperly, eaten by deer, damaged by frost, dried up by drought, choked by overgrowth or destroyed by insects. Only about 800 of those seedlings will survive.

Q: When will those seedlings be ready for cutting?

A: Depending on the type of tree and the growing conditions, it can take anywhere from 50 to 120 years. We've been trying to speed up the process by thinning the forest so the strongest trees get the most light and food.

What's best for the forest?

Natural forests are made up of many varieties of plants and trees. The trees make oxygen for the environment, anchor the soil and provide homes and food for birds, insects and wildlife. Falling leaves and old trees decay and put nutrients back into the soil.

When forest farmers cut large forests, the environment is suddenly changed. The sun dries the earth, the rain may wash soil away, some animals and insects may die while others thrive. If the forest farmers plant seedlings from one or two fast-growing species, the variety of trees in the forest is diminished. Different plants, insects and wildlife will live in the new forest.

There are other problems, too.

Forest farmers may use pesticides and herbicides to destroy bugs and kill choking weeds. Environmentalists argue that these chemicals kill other useful insects and plants and pollute our air and water. Many environmentalists think we should leave the forests alone. Instead of cutting whole forests and replacing them with one or two varieties of trees, they encourage foresters to cut mature trees from varied forests and let nature take its course. Most of all, they want people to stop using so many paper products, so that fewer trees would have to be cut down. Just using a lunch box instead of a paper bag for lunch would help.

The real Smokey

A strike of lightning or a camper's match on a dry summer day can be the beginning of a nightmare. There are more than 9000 forest fires each year in Canada and the United States. Six out of every ten forest fires were caused by nature...the rest by careless humans.

Smokey the Bear, a poster character, was invented during World War II to remind people to prevent forest fires. But soon after, there was a real Smokey the Bear.

A fire-fighter found a black baby cub with burned paws clinging to a charred tree. After the bear's paws were bandaged, the fire-fighter took a picture and sent it to the newspapers. He thought the picture would remind people about fire safety. People started calling the little bear Smokey and he became an instant celebrity. An advertising campaign with Smokey saying, "Only *you* can prevent forest fires" was such a hit that the number of forest fires caused by humans was cut in half.

Other places have their own "Smokeys" to prevent forest fires. France has a hedgehog, Australia has a koala, Spain has a rabbit, Russia has a moose, Quebec has a chipmunk, Chile has a coypu and Turkey has a stag.

Forest facts

- It takes a forest fire or hot sunlight to open the cones of the jackpine and lodgepole pine to release their seeds. So after a fire there are more of these trees than any other kinds.
- Fire-fighters on the front line of a forest fire have to keep drinking and taking salt to compensate for the 2 litres (2 quarts) of water they sweat out every hour.

- Evergreens do drop their leaves. The leaves, called needles, are shed all year long instead of just in the fall when deciduous trees lose their leaves.
- Giving nature a hand with seed production and harvesting is called silviculture. The word comes from the Latin word for forest (silva), and it is the art and science of cultivating the forest. It's a new science and foresters are just now cutting the first trees planted in massive reforestation efforts. Scientists feel that by using silviculture, foresters can reduce the time it takes to grow forests by 15 to 20 years.

- The tallest living tree in the world is a Sequoia that stands 112.1 m (367.8 feet) high in California. It's estimated that it has enough wood to make 50 six-room houses.

Leaf prints with a difference

If you walk through a natural forest, you'll discover just how many species of trees live together. Collect the leaves and make a collage. Here's a simple way to make permanent prints of what you find so that you're not left with a wilted, crumbling mess.

You'll need:
a table
newspaper
leaves (deciduous and coniferous leaves)
carbon paper
an iron
white paper

1. Cover a table with newspaper for protection.
2. Put your leaves, vein side down, on a piece of carbon paper, with the carbon side up.

3. Cover the leaves with a second piece of newspaper.
4. Turn the iron to low heat. Gently iron the layers.

5. Lift the newspaper and remove the carbon paper.
6. Put a piece of white paper under each leaf. Cover the leaf with newspaper and iron again.

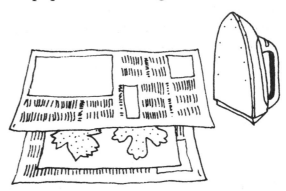

7. When you remove the newspaper and leaf, there will be an imprint of the leaf on the white paper.

Take a tour through a paper mill

1. The essential ingredient
Without these trees you wouldn't have newspaper, or school books, or paper bags, or toilet paper. It took 100 years for these trees to grow and one minute to cut them down. They're called logs now and they're on the way to the mill.

2. Barking
The logs move through huge rings where powerful jets of water rip the bark off them.

3. Chop and mix
The logs are chopped into pieces and combined with wood leftovers such as sawdust and old paper.

4. Ground to a pulp

In about three hours, the skinned logs are turned into pulp either by grinding them or cooking them in a hot, chemical soup, or both. Ground pulp is called mechanical pulp. Cooked pulp is called chemical pulp. Wood is hard to mush up. It's made of stringy cellulose fibres thinner than a human hair and lignin, a natural glue that holds the fibres together. It's the lignin in your newspaper that turns yellow in sunlight. When you break apart the fibres and lignin and add liquid, you have pulp.

6. Whiter, brighter, stronger

The muddy brown pulp is bleached with heat and chlorine or pure oxygen. Mechanical pulp is mixed with chemical pulp for stronger newsprint.

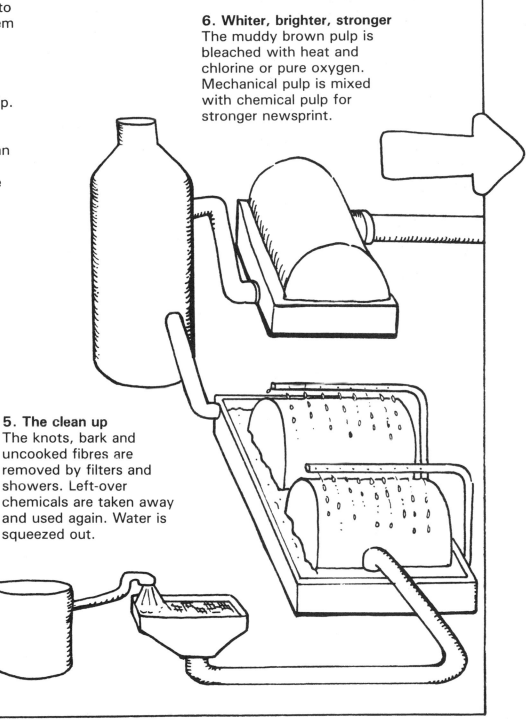

5. The clean up

The knots, bark and uncooked fibres are removed by filters and showers. Left-over chemicals are taken away and used again. Water is squeezed out.

7. Smooth it

The pulp fibres are hollow and stiff. Knives inside a refiner break them up so they'll bond together better. Clay and other additives make the pulp smooth. Computers take the guesswork out of papermaking. They decide the right amount of chemicals and additives to make the perfect paper whether it's for bags or invitations.

8. On the wire

A stream of pulp is poured onto the "wire," which is the length of a football field and two storeys high. The watery pulp is spread out evenly on the wet end of the wire. Water is removed by draining and suction.

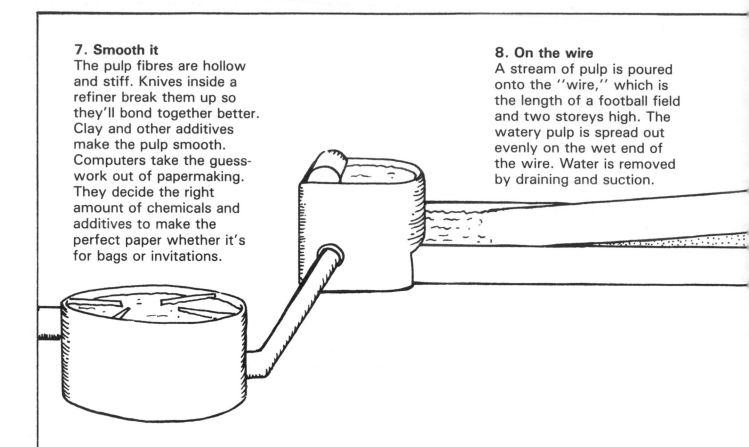

Pulp and pollution

Waste products from pulp mills were once flushed into lakes and rivers. But these "effluents" removed oxygen from the water and harmed plant and wildlife. Today, mills remove fine particles of bark, wood-fibre, lime and other chemicals from the liquid waste and re-use the cooking chemicals.

That has helped, but some mills still have pollution problems. They release chlorine into lakes and rivers. Chlorine bonds with other molecules and becomes a dangerous substance called an organochloride. (Dioxins are the most famous organochlorides.) Using oxygen instead of chlorine for bleaching pulp eliminates this problem. Some mills use aerated lagoons. The effluents flow into a man-made lake where oxygen is pumped into the water and microorganisms gobble up nasty chemicals or change them into harmless products.

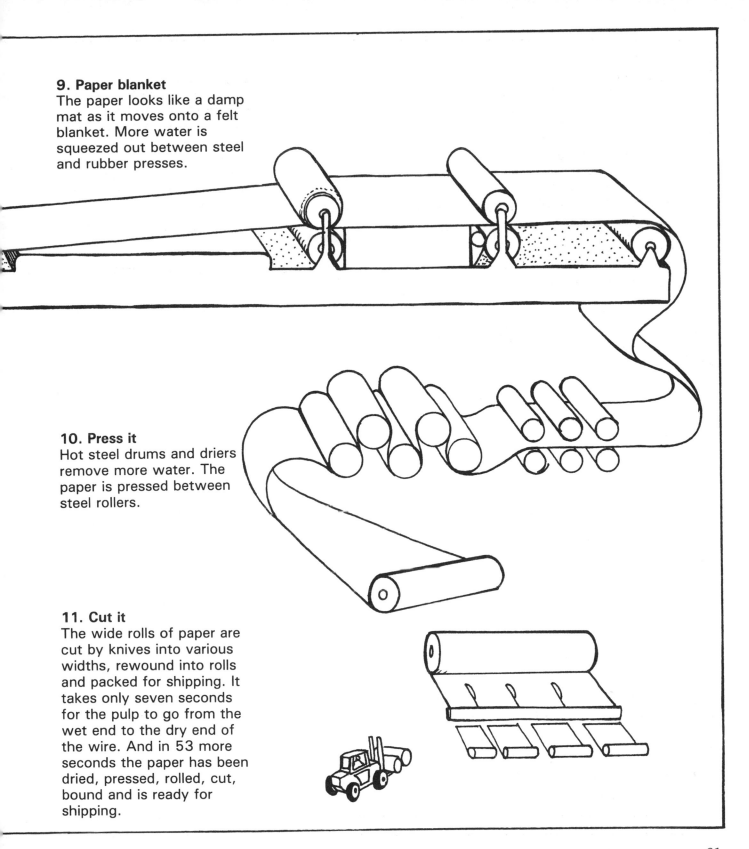

9. Paper blanket
The paper looks like a damp mat as it moves onto a felt blanket. More water is squeezed out between steel and rubber presses.

10. Press it
Hot steel drums and driers remove more water. The paper is pressed between steel rollers.

11. Cut it
The wide rolls of paper are cut by knives into various widths, rewound into rolls and packed for shipping. It takes only seven seconds for the pulp to go from the wet end to the dry end of the wire. And in 53 more seconds the paper has been dried, pressed, rolled, cut, bound and is ready for shipping.

Before there was wrapping paper, people used paint and fabric to decorate containers. The ancient Chinese even used tinsel ribbons on presents. But when the British invented wallpaper in the early sixteenth century, they accidentally invented gift wrap too: people used left-over wallpaper to decorate gift boxes.

While the British may have used wallpaper for gift wrapping, until recently some natives in the South Seas used gift wrapping for wallpaper! Some native peoples believed the images of Santa Claus and his enchanted reindeer were godlike and could ward off evil spirits. Huts all over one small island were decorated with Christmas wrapping.

Here's how to make marble-like wrapping paper that's so colourful you won't need to add ribbons or bows.

You'll need:
3 small jars with lids
paint thinner or turpentine
2 or 3 different oil-based colours (ask if
    there is some left-over house paint
    or use model car paint)
water
a deep pan you can throw away
a stick for stirring
newspapers
white paper

1. In each of the small jars mix an equal and small amount of turpentine or paint thinner and oil paint. Put each colour in a separate jar.
2. Pour about 7.5 cm (3 inches) of water into the disposable pan.

3. Carefully pour one jar of thinned paint into the water. Swirl it very gently with a stick.

4. Add the second jar of paint and swirl very gently. Don't overmix the two colours. They should appear as swirls of separate colours.

5. Add the third jar of paint and swirl gently.

7. As soon as the entire paper is wet, take it out and let the excess paint and water drip off into the pan. DON'T LET IT SOAK.

6. Float a sheet of paper on top of the water. Almost instantly the bottom surface will be covered in the swirls of paint.

8. Lay the paper flat on newspapers to dry.

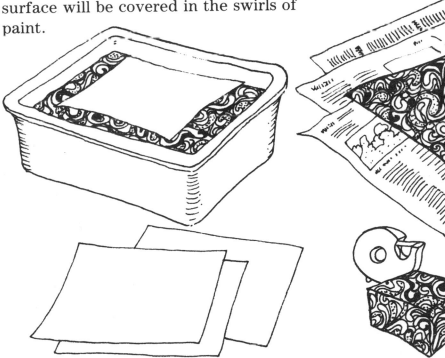

Making a newspaper

Bet you know the answer to this riddle: "What's black and white and red all over?" It's a newspaper, of course. But what else do you know about newspapers? Do you know that a paper like the *Toronto Star* uses 140 rolls of paper each day. Altogether these rolls weigh as much as 35 elephants. An even bigger paper, the *New York Times*, uses four times that many rolls. No wonder newspaper printing presses are a city block long and two storeys high — they're carrying a big load.

Here's how your newspaper is put together every day.

1. Reporters get the story and write it; photographers take pictures. Editors check stories and decide what news goes where in the paper. Ads are drawn. The paper buys some cartoons and columns from syndicates.

2. The story is sent by computer into a typesetting machine. The typeset story comes out in long sheets. Compositors paste ads and daily features onto "dummys". Typeset news is arranged in empty spaces.

3. A camera takes pictures of the finished pages and a computerized machine turns the film into printing plates.

4. The printing plates are put onto the printing press and coated in a thin layer of ink. When the presses roll, the paper moves between the plates and the news is printed on both sides of the paper.

5. The presses fold and cut the papers. Papers are stacked, loaded onto trucks and sent to newspaper carriers, stores and corner boxes.

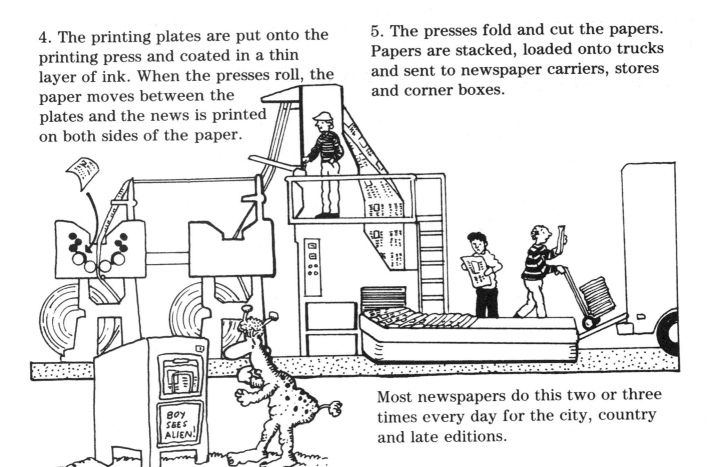

Most newspapers do this two or three times every day for the city, country and late editions.

Did you know?

- The paper used for newspapers is called newsprint, the paper for boxes is called paperboard and the paper for everything else is called kraft paper. Newsprint has to be cheap to make because millions of newspapers are made each day. It has to be easy to fold yet sturdy enough to roll through the presses. Kraft paper is more expensive to manufacture because it must be whiter, stronger and smoother than newsprint.
- In one year, the Elk Falls Mill on Vancouver Island uses enough wood chips to fill three domed stadiums! If you rolled out all the newsprint made by Elk Falls Mill in one year it would wind once around the equator!
- Most newsprint is made from sawdust, wood chips and recycled paper.
- Paper has 15 percent water content. Paper would crumble and crack if it didn't have some moisture.
- Finished newsprint is wound onto giant rolls that can hold enough paper to publish 50 000 copies of a newspaper.

Second-hand paper

Stop! Don't throw out your boxes or newspapers. Recycle them — you might save a tree and save your world from becoming one giant garbage heap.

When you throw newspapers and cardboard into the trash, it is collected and taken to a huge, empty lot and buried. Governments are running out of places to bury garbage. Burning paper isn't the answer because that pollutes the air.

If everybody cut down on paper use (why not take a lunch box to school instead of brown-bagging it?) and recycled paper, half of all the garbage in land-fill sites would disappear!

Fortunately, more people are getting on the recycling bandwagon. Most communities collect old newspapers and

corrugated boxes to recycle into newsprint or cardboard. Most companies shred old paper for recycling. The results are showing: five percent of all new newsprint is made from old paper.

Recycling isn't a new idea. The first recyclers were ancient Egyptians who poured liquid over old papyrus sheets to get rid of ink and then used the sheets again. In the late seventeenth century, the Danish invented a de-inking solvent (something with the power to break apart bonds such as the bond between the ink and the paper). Today paper from all sources — computer cards, food packages, cheques, envelopes and note paper — is de-inked and made into pulp. The paper made from this pulp is so close to wood-fibre paper only an expert can tell the difference.

Newsprint cannot be recycled into top quality writing paper. So what happens to the old papers you leave by the curb for recycling? They become shingles, roofing materials or insulation.

Here's something that's hard to believe. Sometimes there is too much recycled paper around and it's wasted. There isn't a big demand for recycled paper products. If you insisted on using only recycled paper products — and your friends and family did the same — the demand would grow.

I would like to buy a card printed on recycled paper.

Cards Cards Cards

Now that's recycling!

Elis F. Stenman is the king of newspaper recyclers. For 20 years, Mr. Stenman rolled sheets of newspaper into tight little cylinders 1 cm (½ inch) thick and made them into furniture. He even made a piano. When Mr. Stenman made a cottage in Rockport, Massachusetts, he used regular wooden beams, but everything else was made of paper. He made each wall and ceiling board by layering 215 sheets of newspaper and glue.

Make your own de-inker

Most recyclers just want to dissolve the ink on paper so that they have a clean sheet to make into pulp. But you can also lift an entire picture off a page with this home-made de-inking solvent.

You'll need:
125 mL of water   ½ cup
30 mL of turpentine   2 tbsp
a drop of liquid soap
a small container with a lid
a paint brush
a picture or cartoon from a magazine or
    newspaper
2 pieces of clean white paper
a spoon

1. Pour the water, turpentine and soap into the container. Cover tightly and shake well.

2. Paint over your picture with the mixed-up solvent.

3. Put the picture face down on a sheet of clean, white paper. Put another clean piece of paper on top like a sandwich.

4. Use the back of your spoon to rub the top piece of paper. Rub hard and the entire picture will transfer onto the bottom sheet.

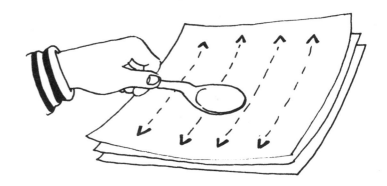

5. Peel the top and middle sheets off.

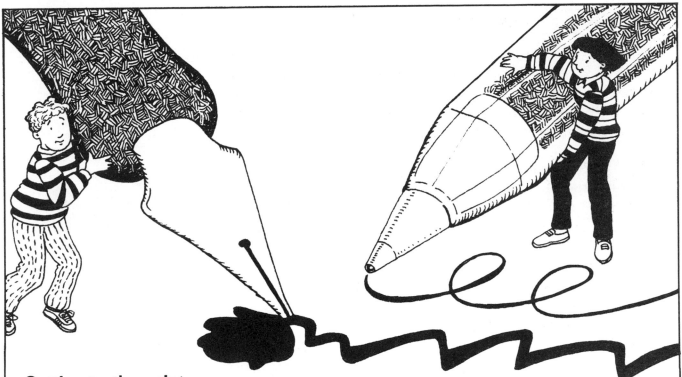

Getting to the point

Ask your grandparents how they learned to write. Chances are they'll tell you about dipping their nib-tipped fountain pens into ink pots on their desks. Fountain pens weren't much fun. They had to be refilled often and the ink took a long time to dry so it smudged a lot. Now people use ball-point pens; they're cheaper and easier to use than fountain pens.

The first ball-point pen was a failure. Lazlo Biro and his brother Georg designed a pen that used gravity to get the ink to flow down a tube onto a roller ball. The pens had to be held upright to work and the flow of the ink was unpredictable — sometimes it was too slow, other times it was gloppy. Biro then designed a pen that depended on capillary action — that means the liquid creeps into small places. Biro's invention had a tube of ink feeding into a smaller tube with a ball at the end. It didn't matter if the pen was held on an angle, or even upside down — the ball was always wet with ink because of capillary action.

Unfortunately, Biro's pens leaked and smeared ink. In 1949, an American, Patrick Frawley, invented a retractable pen with no-smear ink. It was a hit. And in 1952 Marcel Bich of France designed cheap clear plastic pens and — you guessed it — the "Bic" was born. At least the English haven't forgotten the origins of the ball-point pen — they call them Biros.

Neat thing to do with paper # 6: **Make a party of it!**

You can always recycle newspaper by making it into art. How about a piñata? For birthdays in Latin countries, kids celebrate by being blindfolded and wielding a stick until they hit and break open a colourful papier mâché piñata suspended from a ceiling or tree branch. Goodies come crashing down. Use your imagination to come up with a creature — how about an alien piñata or a prehistoric piñata? You can also use papier mâché to make great masks for decorating your room or wearing to costume parties.

You'll need:
newspaper
scissors
a balloon
string
a deep bowl
flour and water mixed together to
    make a glue
paints and scraps for decorating
a sharp knife or Exacto cutter

1. Cut the newspaper pages into 5-cm (2-inch) wide strips.

2. Blow up the balloon. Tie with a double knot.

3. Dip the newspaper strips into the paste one strip at a time.
4. Cover the balloon with the newspaper strips. Overlap the strips and make another layer. Make four layers in all.

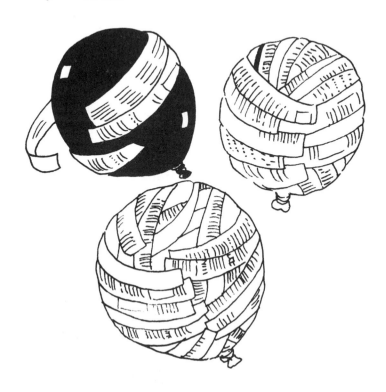

5. Let dry for about a week or until the papier mâché is hard.

6. Decorate the piñata any way you like with paints, feathers, odds and ends.

7. Cut a hole in the top of the piñata. Pop the balloon and remove it. Stuff the opening with goodies (small toys or wrapped candies are good).

8. Hang the piñata by attaching a string with glue or tape. Blindfold your guests, give them sticks and let them start swinging. Watch out!

How wood is made

Just under the bark of every tree is a layer of cells called the cambium. It is only one layer thick but there would be no tree without it — the cambium manufactures the wood and bark.

Cambium cells make phloem. These are hollow cells connected together from the tips of the roots to the tips of the branches. The food and oxygen made by the leaves flow through the phloem to the roots. Old phloem cells on the outside toughen to become bark.

Cambium cells on the inside become sapwood. Sapwood carries the tree's sap (mineral-rich water) from the roots to the leaves. (Maple syrup is just maple sap boiled until it's thick.) As more cells are made, the old sapwood gets clogged with minerals and hardens into heartwood.

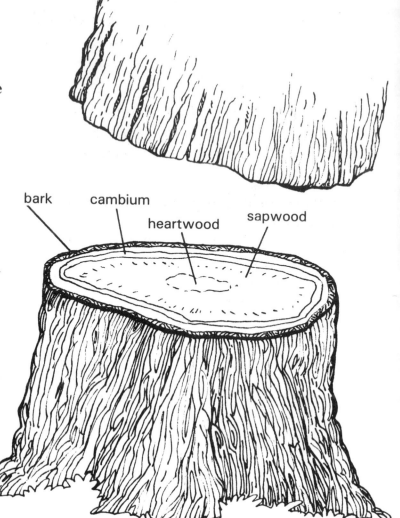

bark   cambium   heartwood   sapwood

Reading the rings

During spring when there is lots of growth, trees make light-coloured wood. In summer when the tree grows more slowly, it makes dark wood. When a tree is cut, the dark wood appears as a ring. Counting the rings lets you know how old a tree is. A knot in the wood is formed when a bud on the tree trunk grows into a branch.

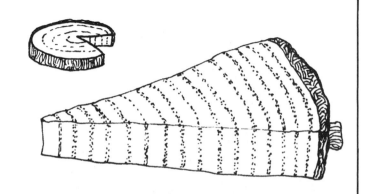

Neat thing to do with paper #7: Which paper towel is best?

You've probably seen ads for paper towels. Each manufacturer claims its paper towel is the most absorbent. Do your own consumer testing and see.

You'll need:
5 sheets of paper towel, all different brands
water
a small bowl
food colouring
an eye dropper
a ruler

1. Put the paper towels in a row.
2. Put some water in the bowl and add a couple of drops of food colouring.

3. Using your eye dropper, put one drop of coloured water on each piece of paper.

4. Measure the diameter of each water mark. The paper towel with the largest and flattest water mark is the most absorbent.

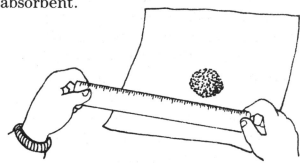

5. Try the experiment again using different kinds of paper — try Kleenex, blotting paper, newspaper and paper diapers.
6. Look to see the different shapes the drops take on once they've been dropped on the paper.

How does it work?
Molecules of water usually stick together when there is nothing else around. But water is fickle. It likes surfaces, especially surfaces with lots of holes, dips and valleys. Absorbent paper is very porous (full of holes). When water hits an absorbent surface such as a paper towel, it spreads out looking for more surfaces. But when water touches paper that is more tightly woven, it sticks together in a beaded drop.

Neat thing to do with paper #8: **Personal puzzles**

You can surprise your friends and family by making them a puzzle they could never buy in a store.

You'll need:
a photograph (try having a favourite photo blown up — pictures of family or pets are great!)
a piece of cardboard cut to the same size as the photo
glue
scissors

1. Glue the photo to the cardboard.

2. Draw two parallel, wavy lines across the back of the carboard.

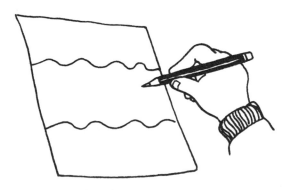

3. Draw lines to intersect the wavy lines. The more lines you draw, the more complicated your puzzle becomes.

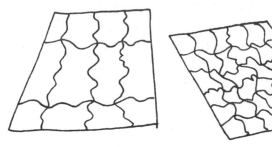

4. Cut along the lines.

You can scramble your puzzle pieces and put them in a box. Wrap the box and wait for the puzzled reactions.

The simplest invisible ink is lemon juice. Dip a toothpick or cotton swab in lemon and write your message on a piece of paper. It will be invisible when dry. Hold the letter close (not so close it burns!) to a light bulb. The letters will gradually show up again.

Why does this happen? The part of the paper with the juice writing will burn faster than the rest of the paper. When you hold the paper near heat, the lemon writing chars and becomes visible. Here's another invisible ink recipe.

You'll need:
a kettle
125 mL boiling water   ½ cup
3 bowls
2 mL cornstarch   ½ tsp
filter paper
a cotton swab
paper
50 mL tincture of iodine   3 tbsp
   (buy this at a drugstore)
100 mL cold water   6 tbsp

1. Pour the boiling water into a bowl, add the cornstarch, stir and let cool.
2. Hold the filter paper over a clean bowl. Pour the cornstarch-water mixture through the filter paper into the bowl. Throw out the filter paper.

3. Dip the cotton swab into your cornstarch ink and write a message on paper. When your ink dries, the message will disappear.

4. Mix the iodine and cold water in a bowl.
5. When you want your message to reappear, swab some of the iodine mixture over the paper.

Why does it work? Iodine reacts with starch to make a purple colour.

Answers

Secret Chinese messages, p. 29
mountain + water = landscape
fire + mountain = volcano

One day two people climb down the mountain.

Making cubes, p. 37
There are 11 possible ways to arrange the squares to make a cube.

Building a better bridge, p. 39
These three bridge designs are the strongest and will support the most pennies.

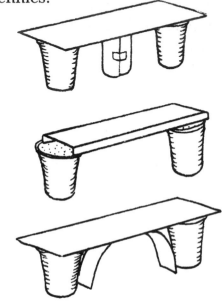

Glossary

Bacteria Microscopic one-celled organisms. They may cause disease or decay or make chemicals change from one thing to another.

Cambium A layer of cells between the bark and wood of a tree that divides to form the wood cells on the inside and the bark cells on the outside.

Cellulose A fibre made of glucose (the sugar food made by the leaves) found in every plant.

Clear cut A way of cutting down forests. All the trees in a large area, except the saplings, are cut at one time.

Conifer A tree that has cones. Cones are hard, protective containers for seeds.

Deciduous A tree that sheds its leaves every year.

Deckle A frame that holds a paper mould in place.

Duff The layer of fallen leaves and wood on the forest floor.

Dibble A tool used for planting seedlings.

Effluents Liquid sewage or waste water.

Environmentalists People concerned with the protection of the environment.

Fibres In plants these are thread-like pieces of cellulose.

Fertilize The joining of male cells with female cells for reproduction. In plants, reproduction means producing seeds; in animals and people, reproduction means making babies.

Humus A thin layer of top soil that is rich in nutrients.

Lignin A natural glue in wood that holds wood fibres together.

Mould In papermaking a mould is a frame with a screen for separating plant fibres from water.

Nutrient Food that helps plants and people grow and stay alive.

Organochlorides These are made when chlorine and organic compounds join together. Organochlorides can cause pollution.

Papyrus A marsh grass (reed) used by the ancient Egyptians to make a type of paper.

Parchment A writing surface made from animals' skins that had been cleaned, dried and smoothed with a stone.

Phloem Hollow cells connected together from the tips of the leaves to the roots of trees. They transport food and oxygen made by the leaves to the roots.

Pulp A soft mush of crushed, wet fibres.

Recycle Using a product or a container again for the same or a different purpose.

Reforestation Planting new trees when forests are destroyed by fire, insects or cutting.

Regenerate To bring new life to something. To reproduce with new growth.

Renewable This means something can become as good as new again. A forest can be totally reborn, or renewed.

Skid A road made of short logs laid side by side.

Skidded Transporting logs by pulling them along a skid road.

Slash The tops and branches of trees that are cut and left on the forest floor when trees are felled.

Species A group of similar animals or plants that can breed with each other.

Toxic chemical A poisonous chemical.

Vellum A fine writing material made from the skin of calves.

Index

absorbency, 73
air pressure, 36
alphabets, 13, 14

bags, brown paper, 19
ball-point pens, 69
bark, 11, 72
bark beetle, 53
berries, to make ink, 11
bleaching pulp, 59, 60
block printing, 14, 24
books invented, 9
bridges made of paper, 39
Bunyan, Paul, 48
burning point of paper, 17

cambium, 72
carbon paper, 20
cardboard, 21, 66, 67
cartons, 21, 37
cellulose, 27, 59
cheques, 16
Chinese inventions, 13, 14,
    16, 25, 29
chlorine, 60
Christmas cards, 20
clay, writing on, 8, 12-13
cloth, to make paper, 9, 28,
    32
clothing made of paper, 19
comic strips, 21
compression, 39
cooking with paper, 17
copying books by hand, 9, 14
cranes made of paper, 40

de-inking, 67, 68
deciduous trees, 56
diapers, 19

Empress Kokan, 24
evergreens, 56

farming forests, 51-54, 56
feathers as pens, 10
flexure, 39
folding paper, 35, 40-41
forest fires, 55, 56
forestry, 42-45, 50-54, 56

fountain pens, 13, 69

Gutenberg, Johann, 15

herbicides, 54
hieroglyphs, 13

ideographs, 12, 13
ink, 9, 11, 13, 75
    make your own, 11
insects and trees, 53
invention of paper, 8-9, 25
invisible ink, 75

Kleenex, 18
kraft paper, 65

leaf prints, 57
lignin, 59
logging, 42-45, 50-54
lumberjacks, 42-48

making paper, 9, 25, 28,
    32-33, 58-61
    make your own, 26-27
maple syrup, 72
Marco Polo, 16
money, 16
movable type, 14, 15
Mufferaw, Joe, 46-47

natural forests, 52, 54, 57
newspapers, 20, 64-65, 66-67
newsprint, 59, 64, 65, 66-67
nut shells, to make ink, 11

origami birds, 40-41

paper cuts, 37
paper mills, 58-61
paper money, 16
paper towels, 73
paper wasps, 30-31
paperboard, 65
papyrus, 9, 13, 14
parchment, 8, 9, 14
parchment paper, 17
pens, 9, 10, 13, 69
pesticides, 54
phloem, 72
piñatas, 70-71
pine cones, 56

pioneer loggers, 42-48
pollution, 54, 60
printing, 14-15, 24
printing press, 9, 15
pulp, 25, 27
    from cloth, 28, 32
    from wood, 9, 32-33, 59,
        60
pulp paper, 9
puzzlers, 34-39
puzzles, 74

quill pens, 10

rags, to make paper, 9, 28, 32
recycling, 66-67
reeds,
    as pens, 13
    to make paper, 9, 13
roots, to make ink, 11

sapwood, 72
scrolls, 14
Sheng, Ch'ing-li Pi, 14
silviculture, 56
Smokey the Bear, 55
softwood trees, 45, 52
spruce budworm, 53
strength of paper, 37, 38, 39
supertrees, 52-53

tall tales, 46-48
tissue, 18
toilet paper, 7, 18
tree harvester machines, 50
trees, 45, 56, 72
    logging, 42-45, 50-54
    paper from, 9, 32-33,
        58-61
    rings, 72
Ts'ai Lun, 25

vellum, 8, 9, 14

wallpaper, 62
wasp nests, 30-31
water content of paper, 65
wood, 72
    pulp from, 32-33, 59, 60
wrapping paper, 62-63
writing, 8-9, 12-13, 29

EDUCATION